The Gates of
AURONA

THE
ANGUANA'S
TALE

WRITTEN BY TONYA MACALINO

ILLUSTRATED BY MAYA LILOVA

CRYSTAL
MOSAIC
BOOKS

This is a work of fiction. All of the characters, organizations, and events portrayed in this novel are either products of the author's imagination or are used fictitiously.

THE ANGUÀNA'S TALE
Excerpt: SPINWATCH

For information, address Crystal Mosaic Books, PO Box 1276 Hillsboro, OR 97123

ISBN: 978-0-9981136-3-0

Printed in the United States of America

To the memory of
Shirley Reilley
(1957 – 2015),
the imagination behind Let's Play Toy Store
and a constant source of inspiration
for me as a
mother, entrepreneur, and dreamer.

–Tonya Macalino

This effort is dedicated to
everyone who surprised me;
to staying humble;
and to The Cat that Walked by Himself.

–Maya Lilova

Table of Contents

List of Full Plates

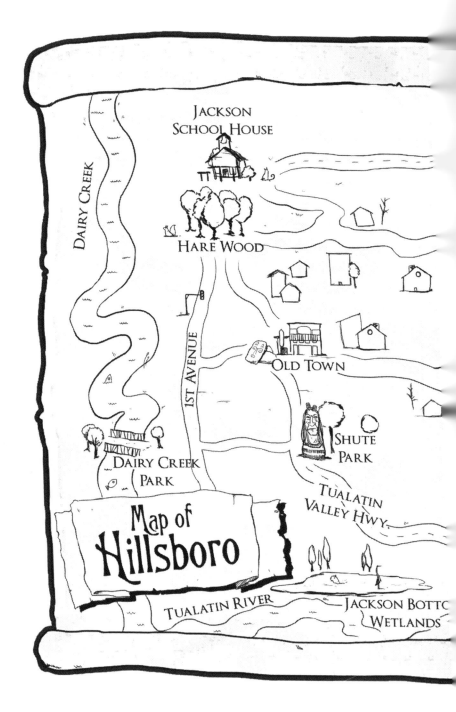

The Gates of AURÒNA

THE ANGUÀNA'S TALE

For Hanna—

Never JUST a kid!

Clang, clang, clang:
The sword against the golden gate.
The treasure waits within.
One treasure brings one heart true love;
One treasure brings the world to end.

Clang, clang, clang:
The sword against the sword.
The guide waits within.
The mother brings the marmot peace;
The father brings the eagle war.

Clang, clang, clang:
The arrow against the shield.
The hero waits within.
The eye of night brings tired-heart peace;
The warrior brings red poppy dreams.

Clang, clang, clang:
The sword against the stone.
The traitor waits within.
The king brings greed's final betrayal;
The prince brings pride's final blow.

Clang, clang, clang:
The trumpet against the bone.
The promise waits within.
The queen brings one eternal hope;
The Fànes will rise once more!

THE PICTURE WINDOW HAD THEM TRANSFIXED.

Chapter One

REALITY IN RUINS

Hannah Troyer rolled the last disk of hot dog around the bottom of what had been a heaping bowl of mac and cheese. The big picture window at the end of the table had her, her brother, Cameron, and her mother, Bridget, silent and transfixed. After so many years of waiting, Big Ben, the tallest, spindliest fir tree in the Hare Wood had fallen.

Not far, thank goodness.

No, his brother and sister trees had caught him—for now.

But the roar and snarl of chainsaws ripped apart the peace after last night's storm and Big Ben's bleeding peak shook with his final moments. Hannah's tummy turned sour over her last bite of lunch and she put her spoon down. Suddenly, Big Ben stopped shaking. The chainsaws fell silent. Mom reached over and put her hand over Hannah's.

Big Ben fell straight down through the arms of his sisters and brothers.

"I guess Spinning Mule got somebody last night after all," Cam said.

Mom reached across the table and put her other hand over Cam's, too.

"Spina de Mùl," Hannah corrected. She'd been watching the windows for the rotting mule sorcerer in his blue bath robe all

I GUESS SPINNING MULE GOT SOMEBODY!

morning. If she was Dolasílla, then that made the scary guy from the woods her arch-enemy. She was pretty sure kids her age weren't supposed to have arch-enemies.

The image of Rebekah and Asia conjuring new lies about her behind her back—Medusa hair and head lice and crushes on Adrian—flickered through her head. Her cheeks flushed even though the two girls were probably halfway to Disneyland by now.

Well, not destroyer-of-kingdoms arch-enemies, anyway.

The chainsaws shrieked again.

Mom pulled her hand away; her chair groaned across the floor as she stood up.

"I think it's time to get out of here. Come on. Up, up, up!"

She clapped her hands until both Cam and Hannah got up and dumped their dishes in the sink.

"It's a gorgeous day outside. I've got some photos to shoot downtown and we can swing by the toy store. Maybe we can even get a treat to celebrate your first day of summer break."

Hannah hesitated.

"But what about Spina de Mùl?"

Mom shrugged. "The storm is over and apparently we have a squirrel army—"

"Congress of Marmots," Hannah corrected.

"—Congress of Marmots protecting us. I think we're safe for now."

After a relay of water bottles, bags, and shoes, the three Troyers stepped out into the midday sun. A miniature squirrel did a back flip in Hannah's chest at the "thunk" of her mother locking the door behind them. She took a deep breath and followed her mom down to the sidewalk.

Diana and Clark's minivan was missing from their driveway, but on the other side, Jemma and Odessa, their babysitter's moms, attacked their normally picture-perfect front garden with sharp tools. Apparently, Big Ben wasn't the only victim of the storm.

"Where you guys headed off to?" Jemma asked, waving a pair of garden shears exactly like the ones Hannah kept in her bag to trim her not-so-secret-anymore bower.

"Just into town to take a short break. I've got an article due by tonight," Bridget replied.

"What's this one about?" Odessa asked.

"Just more for the Hillsboro history series. Railroads and steamboats, all that."

Bridget didn't stop walking as she answered. Hannah glanced over to Cam. What? Mom not stop for a half hour to chat with Jemma and Odessa? Either this was going to be the fastest break ever or...

Or Mom was nervous, too.

Hannah waved back to her neighbors.

For a few seconds they walked on in silence. Then Cam bolted.

Hannah took off after him, her nerves demanding some kind of action. She heard Mom shout behind them, then the sound of her shoes smacking the sidewalk to catch up.

Together they stopped at the place where the neighborhood met the woods. Down the hill where the footbridge crossed Hamby Creek, small trees had split and fallen across the path on both sides.

"Wow," Cam said.

"Yeah," Hannah agreed. "I guess we'll be doing some climbing."

One by one they picked their way through branches that now faced the wrong direction. Hannah pulled a twig out of her black ringlets and trotted forward to where Cam stood at the forest crossroads, looking down the path into the deeper woods.

She stopped beside him.

She knew what was down there.

"Can we, Mom?" Cam asked.

Bridget untangled the backpack from the last of the branches and stumbled over to where they stood.

"Heck no."

Cam wasn't deterred. "Come on, Mom. I just want to see it."

Hannah offered a silent nod. Would there be some sign that it all really happened? Not just the incredible storm, but the other things. The things that didn't seem quite so real in the daylight.

"It isn't that far in," Cam urged.

Hannah grabbed her mother's hand and pulled. Soon they were walking down the narrow dirt path toward The Congress of Marmots.

When they reached the semi-circle of trees, she and Cam broke away from their mother and ran to it, searching for claw marks, fur, anything that would make their memories

true. Hannah ran her hand over the scratchy bark. Just plain ol' tree.

Nothing to remember the story by, the story of the Fànes, the story of Dolasílla, the girl who tried to save the Fànes, but who was betrayed by her own greedy father. The story told by a pair of royal squirrels—their black eyes deep with sadness—about the ancient girl Hannah was supposed to be.

But I'm just a kid!

So was Dolasílla.

Hannah moved to the stump and crouched down.

There it was.

With her small fingers, she reached between the sections of bark and pulled free

A SMALL PUFF OF WHITE FUR.

a small puff of pure white fur. She stared at it, her heartbeat disturbing the quiet.

"But I'm just a kid," she whispered.

Mom came up behind her as she stood up and took the little piece of fur from her. Like the night before, she pulled both Hannah and Cam close to her and gazed up the slender trunks of the trees.

"What in the great green avocado am I going to tell your father?" she murmured.

That, Hannah realized, was a very good question.

A very, very good question.

WEIGH, HEIGH, AND UP SHE RISES!

Chapter Two

Ghost Train

Hannah's mother pulled them from the forest onto the road that led to town, obviously on-purpose forgetting that their legs were shorter than hers. She got both feet on pavement and started belting out a familiar sea shanty,

> "Weigh heigh and up she rises,
> Weigh heigh and up she rises,
> Weigh heigh and up she rises,
> Early in the morning."

Hannah gave her hand a slight tug, but her mom just squeezed tighter and kept singing,

"What shall we do with a drunken sailor,
What shall we do with a drunken sailor,
What shall we do with a drunken sailor,
Early in the morning?"

Hannah glanced over to her brother. To her surprise, he had both of his hands wrapped around Mom's. The first of the old cottages came into view and she was sure he would pull away—that same boy who hid from his friends every day to give Mom goodbye hugs at school—but instead he joined in,

"Weigh heigh and up she rises.
Weigh heigh and up she rises.

Weigh heigh and up she rises.
Early in the morning."

She listened to their powerful voices blend, rising and falling in a comforting pattern from her memory. All those long walks to pre-school, singing about pirates and mermaids at the top of their lungs, because the street was empty and the days were so hot or so cold and because Mom said the songs were supposed to occupy your mind and give a rhythm to your work, so the work would be easier.

"Put him in the long boat till he's sober.
Put him in the long boat till he's sober.
Put him in the long boat till he's sober.
Early in the morning."

THE MAGICAL OLD HOUSES DRIFTED BY.

And maybe because the songs put the happy and the belonging back where there was misery and lots and lots of scared. Hannah reached up and wrapped her other hand around her mother's, too. She watched the magical old houses drift by with their ancient trees and winding paths, the ones they used to plan their fairytale lives in during those daily walks. The fear still had a hook in her voice, but carefully she floated it out, just in time for the end of the song,

> "Weigh heigh and up she rises.
> Weigh heigh and up she rises.
> Weigh heigh and up she rises.
> Early in the morning."

"This is where we saw the bald eagle once, isn't it?" Cam remembered, nodding to the playground-sized yard of a house with tall, old-time windows.

"Yeah, and the deer and her fawn, too," Hannah said.

"And back there was the bunny puddle with its huge ears." Mom pointed to a spot in

a gravel driveway behind them. "Looks like they finally filled it in."

But then Mom cut off the chatting with,

"My Bonnie lies over the ocean.
My Bonnie lies over the sea.
My Bonnie lies over the ocean.
Oh, bring back my Bonnie to me...

"Bring back, bring back,
Bring back my Bonnie to me, to me.
Bring back, bring back,
Bring back my Bonnie to me."

And Hannah was kind of glad she did, because the tight spot in her chest had started to come back with the chatting. This time she let her voice burst free, even as she followed

Cam onto the sidewalk and stepped on the kitty paw prints in the cement as tradition demanded to get her "kitty powers."

Downtown came into sight and with it, the very last verse of the very last song:

"Sailing, sailing over the bounding main
Where many a stormy wind shall blow
'Ere Jack comes home again!"

The song faded away and they crossed over into downtown. And out of the "Between" that they had created with their own magic.

Together, they stepped up to the Main Street crosswalk light with the noise of the traffic and the other people talking as they walked by. The air and the sound had a little unrealness to them for a minute. Hannah closed her eyes and then opened them again, trying to reset her brain.

A block ahead, the ghostly MAX train whirred as it glided off to the next station.

"You know, I always laugh when I see that," Mom said. "You know the Oregon Electric used to have its track along that exact same street a hundred years ago. A hundred years ago! They got rid of it when they finally started getting decent roads out here, first 2x12 wood plank streets, then pavement, and cars could finally

make it to Portland. And now look: here we are back where we started. Come on, I need to get a couple pictures."

They hurried down to the MAX station. Mom unloaded the good camera from her backpack and got into position to wait for the next train.

"I don't get it. Why couldn't people drive their cars to Portland?" Hannah asked, watching her mom remove the lens cap and twist dials on the camera as she aimed it here and there.

"Well, what sort of weather is Oregon famous for?"

"Ah, rain?" Cam replied sarcastically.

"Exactly. And what do rain and a dirt road make when you put them together?"

"Mud?" Hannah said.

"And what happens when you run a car with skinny tires through deep mud?"

"It gets stuck," Hannah realized.

"Not just that, it leaves huge ruts in the road. They would put gravel on them, but you know what the gravel on our garden path looks like by the end of the winter."

"Yeah, like mud with a couple rocks in it," Cam joked.

Mom went silent as her target train came into view. Hannah and Cam watched for cars as Mom ran back and forth, shooting photos and checking her view screen, adjusting the settings, and shooting again.

The ghost train whirred off toward the post office stop and Mom walked back to them, checking her screen.

"There was even a second train—the Red Electric—that used to come right here through Main Street."

"When we had wood streets?" Hannah asked, staring at the road, trying to picture the

straight lines of wood sliced through with railroad tracks. They walked back to Main Street and waited for the light.

"No, a few years after the main roads got paved. They had to rip everything up and lay in a sewer system and everything. These early towns could actually be pretty gross before they got organized and started building infrastructure. Hold on, I want to get a picture here before we go inside."

In the middle of crossing the road, Mom stopped and turned to take a series of pictures of downtown. Hannah tried to picture it through her mother's lens—old buildings with their colorful paint, each with a clever old-time design, each filled with miniature adventures— food, antiques, trinkets, instruments, toys, and

HANNAH COULD SPEND HOURS EXPLORING.

books. Hannah could spend hours down here exploring.

But not if she was flattened by a car.

She and Cam dragged their mother from the road as the cars reminded them it was no longer their turn. Releasing their mother to stow her camera, they raced to the door of the toy store. The window displays were packed with stuffed animals playing with summer toys: shovels, rakes, bug catchers, water sprayers. Hannah used the door handle to swing herself around.

"Come on—. What's that?" Hannah let go of the handle and stepped back out past the awning.

Cam followed her, staring up at the sky.

"Are those hawks?" he asked.

VULTURES. HOW CREEPY.

Hannah squinted at the handful of birds making lazy circles in the sky.

"I thought your book said hawks like to live by themselves," she said. "Mom, what are those?"

Mom stopped in the middle of putting her camera back in her bag and looked up. "Whoa, those are huge! What are you?"

She quickly pulled her camera back out, pinched the lens cap off, and pointed it to the sky. She snapped a few quick pictures. Cam and Hannah crowded around the camera to see.

"Vultures," Cam said. They all looked up and down the street, but nothing lay dead or dying. "How creepy."

"Yeah, no kidding," Mom replied, putting her camera away again. "How 'bout we get inside."

Hannah allowed herself to be guided toward the toy store door, her eyes fixed on the vultures, circling, circling. She glanced at the young frog-foot leafed ginkgo trees that lined the street.

No squirrels.

No cats.

Mom took both of Hannah's shoulders and turned her to face her.

"Hannah, they're just birds today. Go play."

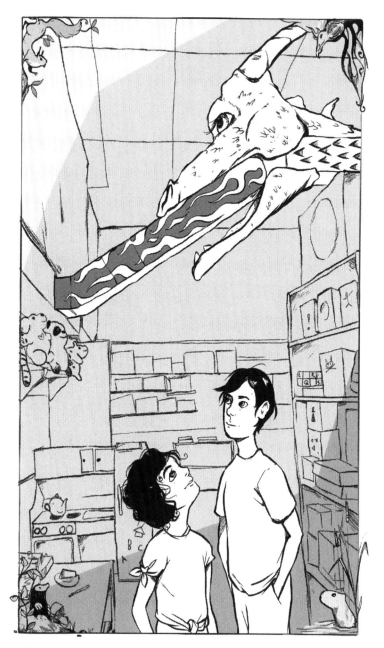

UNDER THE LAZY EYES OF A LADY DRAGON.

Chapter Three

As far as Hannah was concerned, Shirley Reiley had made Let's Play into the awesomest toy store in the universe. Under the lazy eyes of a long, winding lady dragon, the treasure-filled displays made a maze of puzzles and costumes and science kits and art supplies a kid could get lost in forever. And if your mom got caught up yakking with Shirley, you could kill time at the train table or in the pretend kitchen or following the dragon to the end of her long tail.

Hannah and Cam hadn't gotten that far yet.

Mom had given them each ten dollars. They could either each get something small or combine it to get something big.

"Come on, Han! You've already got a million sketch pads at home."

"It's my choice, Cam."

"Look, we could even get a big puzzle. We can do it all together when Dad gets back from Ireland."

Hannah glared. "Dad's around even less when he's home than when he travels." She hugged the sketchpad to her chest.

"Well, then we can do it together. Just you and me." Cam held out the box with the brightly colored wizard surrounded by flying books.

Hannah raised an eyebrow. "So, you're actually going to come out of your room and play with me?"

"Sure. I play with you all the time!"

"No, you don't. You never play with me."

"Come on, Han!" Cam lowered the puzzle and gave her his begging eyes. "Look, if we put our money together and get this, then we'll

have enough left over to get a treat at The Artfull Garden—and we won't have to go back home so soon."

Hannah thought of an ice-cold lavender lemonade for the walk back. But she was no fool. That puzzle would get home and before it was even half done, Cam would disappear with his wizarding books upstairs. She narrowed her eyes.

"Something we can do at The Artfull Garden."

Cam looked longingly at the puzzle, but put it back.

"Hey, maybe a puzzle game," he said, trotting over to a nearby rack. "Look, they even have a travel one about chocolates."

Hannah ran up and took the box from her brother. "Cool! And we'd be playing it at the chocolate shop!"

She went back to put the sketch pad away and followed her brother up to the check-out counter where Mom was deep in conversation with Shirley about business stuff.

"Done so soon?" Mom asked.

"We decided to save some of the money for a treat from The Artfull Garden," Cam told her.

"You don't have to. I'd planned to cover it."

Hannah shook her head. "We know you don't have extra money. This way we won't spend as much."

Mom gave a small, sad smile, then pulled them both in for a hug. "Come on, let's go celebrate properly."

Cam presented their find and their money to Shirley. She took it with one of her pretty, quiet smiles and rang them up.

"This is a great game. You guys going to play this today?"

"Yeah," Hannah said, watching her mother carefully. "We thought it would be perfect for the chocolate shop."

"Absolutely!" Shirley agreed. She handed the turquoise bag to Hannah. "Be sure to say hi to Kay for me."

"Yep."

Hannah and Cam followed their mother toward the door, still waiting to see if their plan would be accepted. Hannah jogged forward to glance at Mom's face. Her eyes were unfocused and her face was soft and empty— the face of someone whose brain was too full.

"Mom?"

"Huh? Yeah?" Bridget fumbled with the door as she pulled herself from her thoughts.

"So can we? Can we stay at The Artfull Garden for a little while?"

"Um, yeah." She leaned into the door and pushed it open with her back. "I have some research to do before I get started anyway."

"Awesome!" Cam shouted as he ran past them onto the sidewalk.

"Not awesome! Holy cow!" Cam stopped in the middle of his dash and looked up.

Hannah and her mom both ran out to see what was going on. They tipped their heads back and Mom immediately pulled them under a nearby awning.

"You do not need faces full of bird splat!"

Even under the awning, Hannah could see that the vultures had invited friends. A big ol' vulture party over old town Hillsboro.

And they were starting to land.

A BIG OL' VULTURE PARTY.

"Come on, let's get across the road," their mother ordered.

Like they were their own flock of birds of prey, they raced down to the crossing and swooped across the street. Vulture feet thumped on the cars beside them as they headed toward The Artfull Garden, three doors down.

The thing with vultures, Hannah decided, was that they were very, very big when they stood on the hood of a car right next to your head. Those pale feet with their claws tapped around on the metal right at the level of her eyes. She stared at them as she speed-walked with her mother, then the ugly red head dipped down.

"Eeep!" Hannah cut off her surprised yelp, slapping her hand over her mouth.

Their hustle halted at the door to The Artfull Garden just as three vultures with huge wingspans landed on the discount tables. A small jar fell from the table, shattering on the sidewalk.

Mom frowned, her eyes narrow. "Okay, you three, off. Off! Shoo! Don't bite me. Or my kids. Shoo!"

Cam grabbed Hannah's sleeve and pulled her behind Mom. Hannah wasn't sure that was better. All the cars along the sidewalk now served as vulture perches.

Of the three vultures in front of the shop, the biggest, shiniest one in the middle now had his toe stuck in a day-old doughnut and

hopped around wildly, smacking his friend with his wing. A coffee cup declaring itself "Mommy's Sippy Cup" was the next to hit the sidewalk. Then an entire basket of discontinued jewelry hit the ground before the dismayed eyes of a cement garden gnome.

Now Hannah's eyes grew narrow. She stepped out from behind her mother and joined her in shooing away the birds.

"Scoot, scoot, stop breaking all of Kay's things!"

After a second's hesitation, Cam joined them.

"Off, off, go on! You don't belong here. This isn't a good place for you. Go on!"

And that's when Hannah made her second observation about turkey vultures: They made very, very loud scary hissing noises like dinosaurs in a grown-up movie. Even Mom jumped as the birds all around them grew angry that they were not welcome.

The three unbalanced birds on the tables gave one last evil hiss and then pushed themselves into the air, the shiny king leading the way.

Hannah, Cam, and Mom dashed for the door and pushed it closed behind them. Kay met them at the front windows, her eyes shocked at the destruction of her discount table.

"What on earth brought those birds down here?" she wondered for all of them. "Should we call someone? Maybe Jackson Bottom? They're going to get hurt."

Mom moved to stand beside her, watching the remaining birds skate awkwardly on the tops of cars, trucks, and vans. They all looked confused, like they didn't know what to do now.

"Do you suppose it's one of those messed up migration patterns like you hear about on the news?" Kay asked, straightening her shop apron as she stood thinking.

"In the middle of summer?" Mom sounded unconvinced.

"True, but with as much as we've messed up the environment, you never know. Well, I might wait just a bit to clean that up. Let a few more of them leave in peace. Anyway," she spun around to face them, "how have the Troyers been?!" She gave Mom a big hug and grinned at Hannah and her brother.

"We are here to celebrate the first day of summer!" Mom announced.

"Well, what can I get you to help celebrate?" Kay asked, walking around the candy counter with its jars and trays of glittering treats to settle back at the espresso machine.

"I'll take an iced mocha. And you two?"

Cam went to the counter and slapped the last of their toy money on the counter. "We'd like a lavender lemonade."

Hannah pulled two dimes from her pocket and set them on the counter next to the dollar bills. "And two taffies."

"Alright then, why don't you two pick your taffies while I get your drinks started?"

"Actually," Hannah said, quickly remembering their tradition now that the vultures had stopped hissing, "could we feed the fish?"

"Is Ollie here?" Cam interrupted, bouncing on his toes.

Hannah didn't wait for the answer, but tossed the toy store bag on the table and ran toward the back of the store. She didn't have to go far until she found the great lady, napping amongst the fancy jewelry their mom's friend Kelly made, her reddish gold paws crossed elegantly in front of her. Hannah buried her face in the long, silky fur. Cam began scratching the elderly dog's chin and worked his way up to her ears. Some of the worry holding Hannah's shoulders tight quietly faded. In fact, she very much wanted

THEIR LITTLE TOWN'S MOST FAMOUS ACTRESS.

to fall asleep across the back of their little town's most famous actress.

She was thwarted by Sue and LaVonne. LaVonne begged their pardon as she squeezed past them with a pile of boxes for the storage room, while Sue offered them the coveted lid of fish food.

"It's a good thing you two reminded us or those fish might have starved today," she joked.

Hannah took the lid and reluctantly pulled away from Ollie. She led Cam back up to the front of the store. She did not particularly want to be near the front of the store, but there were fish to be fed.

The three-tiered fountain where the fish swam sat right behind the table Mom had chosen to work on her research. Just before

Kay made the espresso machine roar like a jet engine, Hannah was pretty sure she heard her mother say a word parents aren't supposed to say in front of kids. Hannah and Cam raised their eyebrows at each other as they knelt beside the fountain. They took turns pinching red flakes into the water, watching the little

mouths snatch the flakes away from the surface.

The jet engine cut off.

"Konking acorns! I'm usually really good at this!" Mom banged on the tablet with her knuckle.

Cam got up, leaving Hannah to sprinkle the last few bites of fish food.

"What's the matter, Mom?" he asked.

Mom lowered her voice. "I can't find ANYTHING on that story. *Fire Eagle* brings up a million different pages I'm pretty sure don't have anything to do with old Italian legends. *Congress of Marmots*, nothing. *Spinwatch*, nothing. *Spinning Mule*, nothing."

"Spina de Mùl," Hannah corrected again, standing up. She looked past her mother toward the cars outside. A dark feather spun on the hood of the blue car at the curb.

"They're gone! Look!"

She grinned at her brother and mother. They smiled back in relief.

"Come on, Han. Let's go play our game, so Mom can get her work done."

Hannah raced her brother to their table.

Maybe they were just birds today.

Just lost, confused birds.

Poor things.

WHICH SPOT FOR THE SQUARE DARK TRUFFLE?

Chapter Four

BLACKING OUT THE SUN

Shirley was right. It was a cool game.

Hannah reached for the lavender lemonade, remembered it was empty, pulled her hand back as she stared at the game board, trying to beat Cam in guessing which spot the square dark chocolate truffle would fit in, if the round pink truffle had to go in the center spot.

Cam jumped in his chair, making a horrible shriek as he dragged it forward.

"I've got it! I've got it!" He shifted a round milk chocolate up one square and like magic, the rest of the eight pieces fit in perfect order.

"Dang it!" Hannah cried.

She flipped to the solution page and yep, he nailed it. Eesh. She really needed to concentrate better!

Together they reset the board.

"Wow. When did it get so dark?" their mother muttered, rubbing at her eyes.

Hannah and Cam both looked up, turning in their chairs to look out the big display windows.

Slowly, Hannah stood up.

"Mom."

She could hear her mother getting up from her chair, felt the warmth of her hands come to rest on her shoulders.

"Holy banana," her mother whispered. "Kay! LaVonne! Sue! You've got to see this."

The three ladies ran up to where Hannah and her family stood.

"I didn't even think there were that many vultures left. Oh, my," Sue exclaimed.

"How many do you suppose that is?" LaVonne wondered.

ENOUGH TO BLOCK OUT THE SUN.

Enough to black out the sun.

And then came the shrieking. Squirrels came running down the street, charging up the young trees, bounding up cars. Hannah clamped her hands over her ears. She saw Cam do the same, squeezing his eyes shut as the vultures dinosaur-hissed their replies.

"Mom!" Hannah yelled.

Her mother's cheek pressed to hers.

"What, Hannah-Bannah?"

"Still think they're just birds?"

"No, Hannah-Bannah."

A vulture tried to land on the blue car. The four squirrels on the roof charged its feet. It grabbed one of them, but had to let go when another sank its teeth into a pale ankle. Hannah flinched. She imagined nut-cutting teeth must be crazy sharp.

Cam pulled on Mom's arm. "How are we going to get home?" he shouted.

"Ooooh. Not good." But Mom started packing her backpack. Hannah and Cam followed her lead, scooping the puzzle into its travel bag. Mom took the tied pouch from them and stuffed it in her pack. The three of them turned back to the battle which grew worse and worse outside. Hannah watched a vulture knock a squirrel from the gingko tree and her eyes grew wide.

Kay turned back to see them all ready to head home, but unable to move.

"Oh, no. No, no, no. You three are not walking home in that. I'm driving you. Just give me a second to get my keys."

Hannah grabbed her mother's hand as they followed Kay toward the back of the shop. She peeked past her mom to look at Cam, his face trained forward, eyes big. If there were that many vultures out front, how many would be behind, sitting on Kay's car?

Ahead of them, Kay pulled off her apron and led the way through the doors to the storage area, filled with mysterious shadows in the shapes of ghosts, trees, and nameless things.  Hannah followed her mom inside; Cam led the way past a stack of baskets with grabbing twig arms and a headless wicker mannequin wrapped in scarves. Hannah squeezed her mom's hand.

Opening the door just a crack, Kay peeked outside.

"There's just one. Bridget, why don't you shoo him off while I get the car unlocked. Kids, wait until I tell you and then you jump in the backseat."

"Sounds good," Mom replied. She grabbed a broom from a shadow next to the shelves beside Cam.

Hannah was not at all excited to let go of her mother's hand. Mom gently pried her fingers away. She gave each of them a quick hug and a peck on the head. Hannah grabbed onto Cam's arm instead. As Kay and their mother darted out the door, the two kids moved forward to take their place, peeking out into the rear parking lot.

The bird on Kay's car was smaller, but pretty for a vulture with her blue-black feathers, Hannah supposed. She seemed terribly offended at Mom swooshing a broom at her. She hissed and snapped at the bristles. Hannah heard the clunk of the locks.

"She's not getting off, kids!" Mom opened the door to the backseat with one hand. "Get in, get in!"

Hannah and Cam darted forward, letting the shop door swing closed behind them. The vulture hissed at them. Hannah froze and Cam did, too.

"Go, go, go!" Mom shouted.

The engine on the big car roared, and then it was the vulture's turn to freeze.

"Go! Get in!"

Cam reanimated first, dragging Hannah along with him. They dove into the backseat. Mom slammed the door behind them. Soon, she and the broom were in the front seat next to Kay.

"Seatbelts!" Mom ordered as Kay put the car into reverse.

Hannah was still a little short to ride without a booster seat. She buckled the

SHE'S NOT GETTING OFF!

shoulder belt nervously, feeling the thick fabric across her neck. She sure hoped Kay was a good driver...and that the vultures left the car alone.

Kay picked up speed as she pulled out onto the road.

The claws on the roof scrabbled around...and then were gone.

Hannah ducked to see the small vulture flap away. Probably to report them to the king vulture.

Kay caught the green light and turned away from downtown to head toward their house. Both Hannah and Cam turned to watch the cloud of black feathers that warred with the silver and brown fur over the street behind them.

Kay looked back in the rearview mirror.

"That cannot be normal animal behavior!"

"No, it's not," Mom murmured. "It's absolutely not."

And then it happened. First one, then three, then six birds turned, beginning a lazy sail in their direction.

"Mom!" Hannah hollered.

Bridget twisted abruptly in her seat. "Oh, squirrel nuggets."

"I get the feeling these birds like you guys," Kay joked, pulling into the turn lane.

"Or something," Cam muttered, settling back into his seat.

"Yeah, or something," Hannah agreed.

She shifted to get her neck out from behind

the seatbelt and caught herself from pushing on the back of Mom's seat before she got yelled at. She clasped her hands on her lap and willed the person in the red Smart Car in front of them to *please* take the turn.

"Go, go, go," Cam whispered.

Hannah couldn't stop herself from taking a peek.

"Large, angry birds coming," she explained to the driver in front of them. "Now would be a good time, to—"

They lurched forward. The car had finally taken the turn and Kay was right behind it. The little red car in front of them considered working its way up to twenty-five miles per hour, completely ignoring the mass of black wings casting deep shadows behind them. Hannah's eyes were about to pop out of her head.

And then the shadow caught up to them.

Hannah clutched the seat.

The driver of the little red Smart Car slammed on the gas. Or electricity. Or whatever. All Hannah cared about was getting out of that shadow.

They were nearly to the woods now.

So many squirrels.

Dangling from the branches of the cherry trees that lined the last stretch of sidewalk. Dashing along the power lines overhead. Bounding from branch to branch up the rhododendrons to the droopy bows of the firs.

The sun shone.

"They've stopped," Mom announced, looking at the side view mirror.

Hannah and Cam twisted back again. The perfect flock of pursuers now billowed like storm clouds in every direction. They flopped back down in their seats.

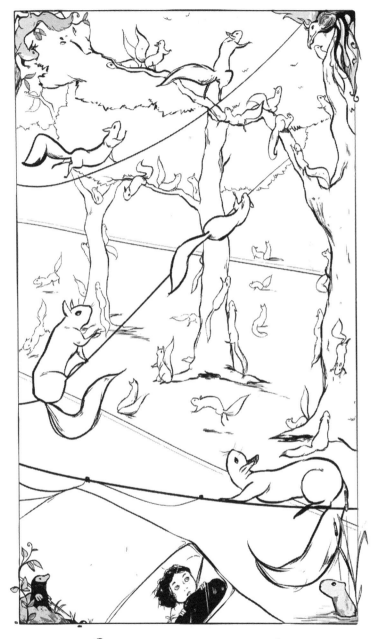

SO MANY SQUIRRELS!

"Turn here?" Kay asked.

Mom guided them the rest of the way to the driveway. Kay settled the car to a stop.

"Wow, well, that was quite the adventure! Holy cow!" she exclaimed.

"Kay, thank you so much for getting us home safely. I guess we really picked the wrong day for a walk," their mother said.

Hannah unbuckled herself and wrestled open the heavy door of the car.

"Kids, what do you say?"

"Thank you!" they both chimed as they scrambled out of the car.

"Lion Kitty! Snowy!" Hannah exclaimed.

The two cats came bounding off the porch toward them, yowling as they went.

As Hannah and Cam crouched over the kitties and reassured them with scratches and strokes, Hannah listened to her mother make her own exit.

"I hope those little rascals let me back into the shop," Kay said with worry in her voice.

"I have a suspicion they'll clear out pretty soon," Mom replied.

"You know something about all this?"

"Not exactly, just a really strong suspicion,"  Mom said in that voice that said she wasn't going to answer your question no matter how much you begged. "Thanks again, Kay."

"No problem!"

Mom pushed the car door closed and Kay backed out of the driveway.

"In the house!" Mom shouted.

They each stood and took one last suspicious look at the early afternoon sky, then darted for the front door.

ALL THE DOORS CLOSED AGAIN.

Chapter Five

POWER OF THE CROSSROADS

Hannah stood alone in the middle of the living room.

She walked over to Nicola's little bed on the couch and rearranged the dried-up funeral roses, purely out of habit.

"All the doors closed again. I miss you, little Nicola. At least you liked to play with me."

She imagined that soft, little black body cuddled up against her, cozy and purring comfortingly. Gone. She wanted to run again, back to her bower, to her safe, secret place. But it wasn't secret anymore, and she suspected it wasn't safe anymore, either. Well, that and Mom had threatened to remove her ears if she went outside.

And she'd kinda looked like she meant it.

Glancing back, she saw that her art stuff still sat on the dining room table. She

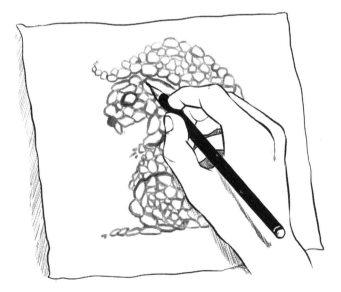

wandered over to it. Picking up a brush pen, she settled on a fresh sheet.

The squirrel mosaic.

Hundreds of small stones—agates and quartz and plain old river rock—all cemented together with thick rich mud. She could practically smell it as her hand moved the pens across the page, first with one color, then another, and another.

Then came the final piece, her dream stone, the eye of the marmot. *The marmot peace.*

"The marmot peace," she whispered, searching her memory.

That chant began its steady beat in her brain, *clang, clang, clang.*

Clang, clang, clang:

The sword against the sword.

The guide waits within.

The mother brings the marmot peace;

The father brings the eagle war.

The eagle war.

The Fire Eagles. The vultures were the Fire Eagles. They'd been allies with the Fànes. They'd taken over from the marmots when the Fànes turned to war. Hannah's eyes got huge.

"Well, this Dolasílla has no intention of going to war!" she declared to the window that looked out over the Hare Wood.

BAM!

Hannah whipped her head around to see Mom's office door slam open. Mom's eyes narrowed and her cheeks sucked in the way they did when she found out you'd spent the whole day "cleaning" your room—by sort of playing with things instead of putting them away. Right then, Hannah wondered if the poem didn't have things backwards, because it pretty much looked like the mother was about to bring the "eagle war."

Hannah screwed up her courage and opened her mouth.

"What, Mom?"

"I cannot write this article series by hiding in this house and we cannot eat, if I do not write this article series! Pack your backpack and tell your brother we are leaving. Get a snack and your water bottle!"

Mom had stormed back into her office mid-speech, leaving Hannah staring at an empty doorway. Her thinking brain knew that this was true: all of the grocery money came from her mother's paycheck. Her oh-my-gosh-I'm-never-going-out-there-ever-again brain REALLY didn't care about food right now.

But she heard her mother stomping around inside her office and sooo did not want to get caught just sitting here when she came back out. Hannah pushed off the chair, ran up the stairs, and banged on Cam's door.

"Mom says to pack a snack and your water bottle. We're leaving!"

Cam poked his head out in just seconds.

"Are you kidding?! Those squirrels and vultures were tearing each other apart out

ARE YOU KIDDING?

there. I don't want to get in the middle of that again!"

"She can't finish the article, if we don't leave. And, well, we're kind of out of groceries," she replied.

Cam's eyes got wide; then he slapped a hand over them.

"This is insane."

Hannah shrugged. It was much easier to

be brave when she was delivering the news than when she was receiving it. "What are we supposed to do, just hide in here forever? This is Blue Bathrobe Man's mess, not ours."

"I don't think the mess cares who it belongs to," Cam grumbled, but he grabbed his wand and came with her.

When they didn't beat Mom to the car, she started snarling. Now was one of those times when Dad would have said that Mom's Irish was showing, and she would have shouted back that it was Scottish, not Irish, and then holler that that was a fine glass house built by a melodramatic Italian and just how long did he plan for it to remain standing?

Where was Dad when you really needed him?

But finally the SUV was rolling backward down the short driveway with all three of them paying more attention to the sky than the road. Snowy and Lion Kitty came bounding down

UNHAPPY WITH THEIR LITTLE REBELLION.

from the porch, obviously unhappy with their little rebellion. Cam waved and said a quiet, "I'm sorry."

Hannah hoped that that was all they were.

To get to the road to Forest Grove, the Troyers had to pass dangerously close to the edge of downtown.

"Keep back from the windows," Mom warned.

Hannah and Cam ducked toward each other, peering with one eye over the backseat. A few vultures remained circling the old town. No, not vultures.

"Fire Eagles," Hannah whispered to Cam.

"What did you say?" Mom asked, her voice slightly less grumpy.

"Fire Eagles. And two of them are heading this direction."

Both Cam and Hannah dropped their heads below the back of the seat.

"Those are the Fire Eagles? There's nothing eagle-esque about them. They were hideous! Well, the one on Kay's roof had pretty feathers, but—how did you decide this anyway?" Mom demanded.

"Clang, clang, clang:
The sword against the sword.
The guide waits within.
The mother brings the marmot peace;
The father brings the eagle war."

"Ah," said Cam, "so we met the 'marmots' last night. Now we've met the 'eagles.'"

Hannah shrugged. "That's what I figured, anyway."

Mom nodded as she looked at them through the rearview mirror. "That poem.

You recited some of it last night. Where did you hear that, again? You can sit up. The 'eagles' are gone."

Hannah stretched as she and Cam straightened in their seats.

"The Blue Bathrobe Man. When I was in my hiding place and he found me the first time, he said this whole big long poem. I can't remember all of it. Just bits and pieces. It had all this stuff about treasures and traitors and how the Fànes will rise once more. It was kind of cool and kind of creepy both at the same time."

"Cool! Maybe you should write it down as you remember it. Then we can ask Dad about it when he gets back," Cam suggested.

Hannah's tummy gave a little nervous twist, but she pulled the sketch pad out of her backpack and dug around for a pencil.

In the front seat, Mom pointed out the window to their right. A huge cemetery with a fancy metal sign arching over the entrance declared itself, "Hillsboro Pioneer Cemetery."

"Are there actual pioneers buried there?" Hannah asked, straining against the seatbelt to see the headstones.

"Absolutely. If you watch closely, you can see David Hill's headstone."

"Where? Who's David Hill?" Hannah

narrowed her eyes at the field of stones, scanning as fast as she could.

"Hill's Borough. Hillsboro. Get it? The town founded by David Hill? Clever, eh?"

"I see it! I see it!" Cam pointed it out to Hannah.

Hannah frowned. "It's kinda shiny for a pioneer tombstone."

Mom pulled the car into line for the left turn. She glanced back at them and smiled. "That's because it's from 1930, about eighty years after he died. He was buried without a headstone. The Daughters of the American Revolution helped some local school children hold a coin drive to buy him that one there."

"Wow," Hannah replied, looking at the big piece of carved granite. Kids raised enough money for that? Maybe kids really could do

big things. Although leading an army and leading a coin drive were kind of different.

"Look at that one! Imbrie. Why do I know that name?" Cam dropped back into his seat, puzzled as Mom finally got to take the turn.

Mom laughed and the sound melted the last of Hannah's tension. The last of Mom's

Irish or Scottish or whatever seemed to be put away for now.

"Imbrie Hall, out at McMenamin's Cornelius Pass Road House where the old Imbrie farm was," Mom reminded him.

"Ah." Now it was Hannah's turn to laugh. "Where Dad goes to his CPR classes after work."

"Exactly."

CPR stood for "Cornelius Pass Road" House, a fancy pub by Dad's office, and had nothing to do with saving people from heart attacks—except maybe from the work stress kind. She and Cam exchanged a grin as Mom pulled into a parking lot they hadn't seen before. Hannah popped her seatbelt and grabbed her backpack. A huge green space stretched out before them with a gazebo, a play structure, and even a baseball diamond. Beyond that lay a cozy wood.

"We're here for pictures, not for wandering off," their mother reminded them.

Hannah and Cameron exploded out of the car and out onto the freedom of the lawn. After pausing just a second to check the sky for dark birds of prey, they took off running.

"We're headed to the woods!" Mom shouted after them.

They each took a quick turn on the slide; then ran after their mother toward the entrance to the forest.

As they rumbled to a halt beside her, Hannah looked around. This forest was different than the Hare Wood. The light was still soft, but more of it got through the younger trees. Slender groves called at her to come exploring, but for now her stomach called louder. She dug into her backpack as she followed her mother down the neat trail.

"Real explorers didn't use trails," she grumbled, thinking back to the pioneers at the old cemetery.

"Yes, but nowadays there are so many of us, there would be no more forest at all, if we didn't use the trails," her mother replied.

Hannah thought back to the scarred and battered Hare Wood and the gentle health it had in the Between, and she knew that what her mother said was true. But it didn't stop the trees and their mysteries from calling.

Sometimes living in "nowadays" was really frustrating.

She dug harder for her tub of cereal and finally found it underneath her pencil case. She popped open the crunchy goodness, then stopped.

"Mom, could you take a picture of this for me?"

Mom and Cam turned back to see what had gotten her

attention. A fallen tree concealed a little burrow in the shadows of its bark.

"A fairy house," Cam said, as Mom got the shot for Hannah's art box.

"So what's this place called, anyway?" Cam asked.

Mom recapped the lens and continued back on the forest path. "Just a little further up here and I'll show you."

They followed Mom to a bank of dirt. Hannah stuffed down the last of her cereal, shoved the box back in her pack, and climbed up. Way down in a gigantic ditch, a sluggish creek tried to push its way past the debris that had fallen into its home.

"Dairy Creek," Mom announced grandly.

"Oh." Hannah tried to put some excitement into her voice, but even to her it sounded fake.

"Dairy as in cow?" Cam asked, raising an eyebrow.

"Yeah, the Hudson's Bay Company had a dairy where this creek met with the Logie Trail." Mom paused, looking at their blank

expressions. "The Hudson's Bay Company? The fur trappers were some of the first explorers out here, remember? Beaver trapping to make those fancy top hats?" Mom peered cautiously out over the edge. "If you can believe it, this creek used to run steamboats out to Centerville."

Hannah looked down again.

No, she could not believe it.

"But!" her mother declared. "This is only half the reason we came here."

Mom trotted off down the trail and left Hannah and Cameron to catch up. They came to a stop at a piece of wooden fence meant to keep them from falling into the ravine. Mom made her ta-dah hands.

"Whoa, that's cool," Cam said.

THE CROSSROADS.

Hannah looked over to where the creek would be if she could see it. A beautiful old train bridge shone in the afternoon sun, its elegant beams of dark wood crossing from one secret cloud of greenery to the next.

"This is what replaced those steamboats. It runs to the old mill out by Hagg Lake even to this day. Right here you go from the trappers on horses and canoes to steamboats to the railroad—all in one place, all at a crossroads. People in the old days used to think crossroads were powerful places full of magic and mystery."

Hannah climbed the old fence, trying to see where the creek went under the bridge. "Why?" she asked over her shoulder.

Her mother lifted her off the fence and put her back on the trail.

"Because crossroads are a choice, a chance for change. Do I stay on this path that I'm already on, or do I go a new way? There was also the idea that paths themselves were powerful and that where they crossed, the boundary between here and the 'other' world would become thin. You never know what could happen in a place like that." Mom waggled her eyebrows.

Abruptly she gave a sharp clap of her hands. "Alright, you two stay here for a second while I get some pictures. We need to keep moving while it's still light out."

Freedom!

Hannah scampered toward the trees. It was sort of a trail, she promised her mother silently. She heard Cam run off in another direction. Thin, twiggy branches coated in jagged green leaves draped over the trail, cutting the sunlight into bright beams. She followed the light down into a small dip, then up a steep bank—which she soon realized was the mound that the railroad tracks lay on. Just a few feet beyond, her mother's crossroads began. A prickle of alarm sizzled through her at the thought of being so close to a working railroad track. She took a step back and heard a loud THUMP above her.

She looked up.

A vulture!

He flew straight at her.

Hannah scrambled backward, but the gravely hill was too slippery. She slid, then fell, rolling backwards into the spidery bushes at the bottom. Her elbows started to sting in a bad way, but she twisted to look back for the huge bird.

A SMALL SILVER BOX CAKED IN DIRT.

He was feet away.

Hannah wrapped her arms around her head and flattened herself to the ground. Air pounded against her bare arms and she held her breath.

And pretty soon she couldn't hold her breath anymore. Cautiously, she lowered her arms. The bird was gone. Quietly, she shifted, rolling over so she could push up to her knees.

There, where her newly re-scraped back had been, was a small silver box, dirt caked into its simple, rugged construction. She raised her head in surprise.

And found a tiny squirrel watching her very, very carefully.

WHERE DID YOU FIND THAT?

Chapter Six

Never Suspect the Little Women

"**Where did you find that?**" Cam whispered as they pulled into the parking lot at Rood Bridge Park after the drive across town for Mom's next set of pictures.

"I found it in the woods at Dairy Creek. It was buried in the ground." Hannah peeked under the lid of the silver box. It was filled with toys and tiny gadgets.

"Hannah-Banana! That's a geocaching box. You aren't supposed to take the whole box. Just one toy and then leave one of your own! Mom! Hannah stole a geocaching box!"

Hannah shoved the silver box back into her backpack and zipped it shut. She glared at her brother.

"How was I supposed to know?! I thought it was just a pretty box somebody lost."

Mom swung the car around into a parking space facing the play structure. "Is that what was clanking around in your backpack? Wonderful. Now, we have to find a chance to put it back exactly where it belongs. Well, we won't have time tonight."

Mom killed the engine and the three Troyers pulled on their bags and slid out of the car. Hannah was the last one out this time, moving with careful attention to her two million band-aids—knees, elbows, back, and palms. Another set of shorts bites the dust. She sure hoped Dad's new job calmed down some of the bills soon or she was going to be out of britches!

She pushed the door closed and hobbled toward the green space. Her mother turned back to her and stifled a laugh.

"Come on, old lady. Give me your back pack."

Mom pulled the bag off her shoulder and Hannah found it a little easier to move. Taking her hand, Bridget began to guide them in the direction of the rhododendron garden. Hannah knew that this path would lead them past the gazing pool out to the duck pond. It was a long path. Her knees whimpered.

Mom gave her hand a squeeze. "They'll loosen up as you get to walking."

Hannah didn't believe her.

A few rhodies still bloomed as they passed through the shady garden, their pink and purple trumpets giving the wood a tropical feel. Normally, she would have asked her mom to photograph a few for her, but right now she just wanted to concentrate on the soothing warmth of her mother's hand. It kept her from focusing on the pull and squish of her scrapes as she walked.

"Where are we going?" Cam asked, circling back to catch his mom's other hand for a few minutes.

"To a part of the park we haven't been to before."

"What part?" Hannah pressed.

"The part you haven't been to before."

Hannah growled, but her mom just smiled.

And true to her word, they passed by the gazing pool with its fancy pavilion without pause, then turned left at the lake. A black duck with mandarin orange eyes floated past, then a plainer lady duck with her ducklings. Somewhere a frog croaked. In the stormy season, this was Cameron and Hannah's favorite place to go for walks. They would take their umbrellas and run as fast as they could and then jump and see how hard the wind would pull them.

There would be no running for Hannah today.

But Cam was almost out of wiggle resistance. She could practically feel it through her mother's hand. He grabbed a stick and took off running, whacking branches as he went. Now it was her mother's turn to growl.

Hannah expected her to snarl about running with sticks, but all she did was holler, "Left!"

Cam hollered back, "'Kay!" and kept on running.

Hannah stopped, tears just barely forming on the edges of her eyelids.

Mom looked down, then crouched down in front of her.

"Too much ouchness?"

Hannah nodded. Too much everything.

Mom dropped to one knee and pulled the other strap of Hannah's backpack on. She reached out her arms. Hannah wrapped herself around her mother, tucking her head into Bridget's neck, warm and comforting. Together they rose unsteadily. She knew she

I HAVE A STORY I'VE BEEN SAVING FOR YOU.

was getting too big for this; that Mom would only be able to carry her for a few feet, but she would take every second she could get.

"So, I have a story I've been saving for you. Maybe now would be a good time for it. Whadda ya think?"

Hannah nodded against the softness of Mom's neck.

"So a couple days ago, I was reading about this lady from Hillsboro. Her name was Fern Hobbs. She had a very humble start. Her family moved here because of financial trouble and she had to both work and take care of her younger siblings, but while she worked, she studied law. Eventually she got such a good reputation that the Governor hired her as his personal secretary. This was a really big deal, because it made her the highest paid woman in public service in all of America. A pretty good jump from where she started, huh?"

Hannah closed her eyes and nodded. Her mom continued the story.

"Well, one day there was a big problem in the town of Copperfield. Alcohol was illegal then, and that town not only had a bunch of saloons running, but lawlessness in general was getting out of control. And the city leaders were in on it! Now Governor West was pretty clever. If he'd sent the militia in, what do you think would have happened?"

Hannah pictured an old west town with saloons and rowdy cowboys.

"A big gun fight?" she murmured.

"Exactly. So what do you think he did?"

Hannah shrugged, then bit her lip as the fire on her back restarted.

"Well, he sent Miss Hobbs. She was all of five-foot-four and barely a hundred pounds, a tiny little proper young lady! Copperfield didn't take her seriously at all. They decorated their town like it was parade day. They had no idea who they were up against.

"See, what they didn't realize was that the militia men in a separate train car were there to support Miss Hobbs. Imagine their surprise when those guardsmen followed her off the train! She demanded the resignation of all city council members involved in the gambling and alcohol trades. They declined. So she instituted martial law. Do you know what that is?"

Inside her safe cocoon, Hannah shook her head.

"Well, the National Guard troops took over the city, those militia guys she had with her. They shut down the saloons, destroyed all the alcohol and gambling equipment, and asked everyone to please place their weapons in that box right over there."

NOT A SHOT FIRED.

"And they didn't have a gun fight?"

"Nope. Not a shot fired. Can you imagine how brave Miss Hobbs would have had to have been, how clever she would have to have been to pull that off? She was one amazing lady. And she just kept right on doing amazing things even after that."

Mom's arms trembled ever so slightly. Hannah shifted, so that Bridget could put her down. Mom knelt with her as she slid to the ground and she wrapped her hands around Hannah's shoulders.

"That story made me think of you. Whatever we've gotten ourselves wrapped up in, they can never realize how powerful, how clever, my little Hannah-Bannah truly is." She finished the story by pressing a kiss to Hannah's cheek.

Even as she fit her hand securely back in her mother's and started off to find Cam, Hannah played the story back over again in her mind. She felt both braver and a little more scared. Miss Hobbs had stood up to a bunch of guys with guns, but those guys had gentlemen's rules. What sort of rules did corpse mule sorcerers have, she wondered.

They caught up to Cam on a bridge, leaning out over the railing.

"Get down," his mother said in greeting.

Hannah released her mother's hand and went to stand with Cam, watching the rushing water below. Now *that* was a river.

"Which one is this?" Hannah asked.

"The Rock Creek. I wanted to get some pictures of the confluence, where the Rock Creek pours into the Tualatin, but I asked around and they said the only way you can do that is by boat. They were going to run the trail up there, but when they were exploring to plan the paths, they discovered that not only was the bank dug out underneath, making it unsafe, but that a group of river otters had built their slides and dens down there. And apparently if you try to sneak down there yourself, you'll get covered in poison oak, so I figured I'd get a few pictures here."

"Otters? I want to see an otter!" Hannah exclaimed.

"Yeah, because screaming at the top of your lungs will encourage them to come visit!" Cam teased. "Come on, let's get out of the picture."

Reluctantly, Hannah followed him up the short hill, so Mom could get her shots. The further they got from the duck pond, the more real the forest became, with hanging moss and rich smells of bark and soil. Hannah drew in a deep breath. And then coughed.

And then there was that other smell. Gak!

Something was on the other side of the path's border, and she was pretty sure she knew what. Clinging to a tree, and standing on her tippy toes, Hannah peered over the edge beyond the trail.

"That's the Tualatin," a voice announced suddenly.

Hannah screeched and jumped ten feet into the air. Mom grabbed her, while Cam laughed hysterically.

"Slow down there, flying squirrel," Mom warned with a chuckle.

Hannah recovered her grip on the tree and glared at Cam.

"So can you picture steamboats sailing down that? They had to work hinges into their smokestacks to get under the bridges, but they used to make weekly runs from Lake Oswego along here. Well, sort of Lake Oswego, anyway. You had to take a mule-drawn train from the lake to the river and then continue on your journey. Some people walked, I've heard. Oh, and it wasn't Lake Oswego back then. It was Sucker Lake. For

some reason they changed the name." Mom winked.

Hannah stared at the quiet green water. It reminded her of a miniature Mississippi, slow, stinky, and kind of gross. A new breeze stirred up and tossed her curls in her eyes. She pushed them behind her ear.

"I don't know if I could stand being on that river for very long," Hannah decided.

"Me either," Cam agreed from a tree further down the path.

Mom shrugged. "Part of it is the low water level right now, and, well, there's a waste water treatment plant over there, so that probably doesn't help, but really, I imagine this river looked very different back then. They say before the pollution started that this river used to run silver with the smelt in the spring."

"What are smelt?" Hannah asked.

"Something that stinks. Kidding! They're little fish. Anyway, the steamboats were short-lived here, too. Once the railroad went in, it was over. What was that?"

Mom stepped back down onto the path and Hannah followed her. The breeze had gone straight from gentle to wicked and the trees cracked and groaned. But there was something very not right about the sound coming from those branches.

HE WAS GONE.

"Cameron?" Mom yelled.

Together, the two Troyer girls ran to the bottom of the hill. Hannah saw her brother dueling with a tree branch down on the other side of the bridge.

"That boy's got a short memory," Mom growled.

Then suddenly all the shadows of the woods dropped, dropped, then shot up into the air.

"Mom! The vultures!"

Together they ran toward Cameron who still played swords.

"Cameron!" Mom screamed.

Then a cloud of black feathers dropped around him and he was gone.

THE BLACK CLOUD OF FEATHERS.

Chapter Seven

The Dwarves' Treasure

No amount of desperate screams had brought that black cloud of feathers or her brother back to earth. Hannah could just see it faintly through the blur of her tears, far out on the horizon. Beside her, her mother stood still and pale with her hands wrapped around her mouth.

Hannah's hand shook as she reached for her mother, then she stopped.

"The squirrels," she croaked.

Mom reanimated in a snap, looking all around them.

"Yes, yes, we've got to find them," she agreed.

But Hannah knew they would need more than just common tree squirrels. They would need the squirrels from the Between. They would need magic.

She pulled on her backpack that still hung from her mother's shoulders.

"I have the squirrel's eye in my pencil case."

Moving quickly, they dropped the bag to the ground. Mom held it open while Hannah dug through it for the case, but just as she found it, her hand hit the silver geocaching box. She froze. The knowing came back into her. The same knowing that had been in her

chest and arms, her entire body that night as they hid in the bower and crouched over the squirrel mosaic.

"What? What is it, baby girl?"

Hannah put down the pencil box and instead pulled the sturdy silver chest from the pack.

"It's not the eye this time. This box... Mom, can a path and a river make a crossroads?"

"What? Why does that matter—"

"You said they are magical."

Bridget nodded her understanding, her face growing slightly less pale.

"Let's try it."

Hannah pulled her backpack over one shoulder and with her mother at her side, walked the chest to the center of the footbridge. The chest knew exactly where it wanted to be. Slowly, carefully, she set it down there.

The Troyer women both stepped back.

It began.

Bridget wrapped her hands around Hannah's shoulders as the first tendrils of golden light curled up from the box. The gate unfurled its golden bars like a plant sending up branches and leaves and intricate blossoms.

Hannah reached out and gave it a delicate push.

Her mother followed her through.

THE FIRST TENDRILS OF GOLDEN LIGHT.

The footbridge on this side was a fallen tree. And not a very large one. Hannah and her mother crossed it quickly to the shore. Hannah looked everywhere for a path.

"Where are we supposed to go from here?" she asked in alarm.

Cam, Cam, Cam.

She tried not to think what it must be like for him right now, caught in a cloud of black feathers and claws and dinosaur hisses. It made it too hard to breathe.

Behind her, something rippled through the water.

She turned in time to see that something burst from the creek. At first it appeared to be the sleek, furry head of a river otter, but it changed as the water poured away from it. A beautiful woman, draped in the glittering blues and greens of the waters she protected, stepped from the spray, holding her hands out to them.

"Welcome, daughter of my daughter."

Hannah raised her eyebrows in surprise. The woman smiled.

"I am the anguàna of the lake below the mountain called Croda Rossa. My daughter, the orphan girl Moltina, was the first of your noble line. It was she who learned the language of the marmots, learned to take on their form, joined houses with them and made

WELCOME DAUGHTER OF MY DAUGHTER.

them protectors of your people. These are your gifts as well."

Mom pulled Hannah close.

"We come begging for your help, Lady Anguàna," Mom said in a strange formal tone. "My son, her brother, has been taken by the Fire Eagles."

The anguàna bowed her head in acknowledgement.

"Your house also bound themselves to the Fire Eagles. With each generation, the binding is sealed with an exchange of the twins. The marmots trade a pup for one of your princesses. The eagles trade an eaglet for a prince. This is done to ensure the continued loyalty of the houses."

The anguàna's arms moved gently, fluidly as she spoke. It took Hannah a moment to realize what she meant.

"What?!" she exclaimed.

"They are going to keep him?!" Mom said in utter disbelief.

"When they came to renew the pledge, you sent them away, rejected them."

Hannah thought back to when they were shooing the vultures off of Kay's discount tables and how confused the birds had looked as they'd flown away. Her eyes grew wide.

"Please, how do we get him back?" Mom begged, flicking away tears.

The anguàna glided forward.

"Do not grieve for your son. He is not harmed, but raised as their own."

"What? They kidnapped him! I want my brother back. How do we get him back?" Hannah shouted.

The anguàna became very still, very quiet. Through Hannah's anger a small crack of panic grew wider, more jagged. Had her shouting offended the lady? Would she decide not to help them? Hannah wrapped

her hands around her mother's where they rested on her shoulders.

Finally, the anguàna spoke. "I understand that this is no longer the way of your people. Perhaps if you assured them that the pledge is still strong between your two peoples. But they are a warrior race; pretty words will not be enough. You must show them you are warriors as well."

"How do we do that?" Bridget asked.

The anguàna looked to Hannah. "You must return the treasure you stole from the cave of the dwarves. It was the dwarves who gifted Dolasílla the silver ingots for her bow, the silver reeds for her unfailing arrows, the ermine skin for her white armor. These you will need if you are to convince them that your house still honors the pact."

"Thank you, Lady Anguàna," Mom whispered.

The anguàna floated forward. "Go quickly, daughter of my daughter. And listen well to the tales of *all* your ancestors. You will require their wisdom, if you are to avoid their same mistakes. Go, go quickly."

She brushed a watery fingertip along Hannah's cheek, then twisted around. Streams of river water and twilight rose up around her as she spun. And collapsed back into the rush of the Rock Creek. A sleek brown head pushed through the water, darting toward the Tualatin. Hannah touched the moisture on her cheek. She pulled her hand away. The water glittered on her fingers.

She and Cam were descended from that?

"Dwarves," her mom said, jarringly loud.

Together they backed quickly away from the bank and began jogging toward the fallen tree bridge.

"Maybe moles or voles or snakes or something?" Hannah wondered.

"Your guess is as good as mine."

One minute Hannah was climbing the tree, the next minute she was standing once more on the footbridge, but as her mind settled back into the real world she saw that her mother had already grabbed the silver box and her hand.

They ran back in the direction of the pond and its trails, splitting up to search the earth for any signs of "dwarves."

"Stay as close to the trail as possible. We don't need to deal with poison oak in the middle of all of this."

"'Kay," Hannah replied.

She scampered ahead to look under the cover of a broken branch which supported a load of moss and sheltered smaller plants beneath it. As Hannah reached to part the leaves, an older couple walked up from where they'd been watching the ducks.

"Did you lose something, sweetie?" the woman asked, her hand resting on the crook of her husband's arm.

Yeah, my brother, Hannah wanted to say, but instead she pushed her face into a smile.

"Nope. Just looking for dwarves."

The man laughed. "Well, that definitely looks like a good hiding place for dwarves! Good luck with your adventure there."

"Thanks," Hannah said and reached back into the leaves.

"Mom! I found one! Mom!"

She twisted around to look for her mother and saw the older couple grinning.

"Congratulations," the old man told her.

"Uh, thanks," she mumbled, relieved when her mother jogged past them and came to kneel beside her.

Her mom stared at the mound of crumbled dirt.

"So what do we do?" she asked. "Dig it out and shove the box in?"

"I guess."

Hannah burrowed her fingers into the loose earth.

It exploded in her face.

THE BOX WAS FILLED WITH SILVER POWDER.

A glossy grey body burst free, leading the way with a tiny pink nose and tiny pink paws. One after the other after the other, five moles scrabbled their way to the surface and surrounded the silver box where Mom had set it down to start digging. Two stood to the side almost like little guards as the other three struggled with the lid. Abruptly, the lid flipped open, taking one of the moles with it. He fell into the box.

But the box was no longer filled with funky toys.

It was filled with silver powder.

A plume of silver flew into the air.

Hannah and her mother pushed to their feet and stumbled back, coughing and wiping at their eyes. Hannah shook her head, her eyes tearing from the grit scratching at them. As the tears cleared a bit of her vision, she could just make out the last of the quick little moles burrowing back into the hill. The box was empty.

Her mother brushed at Hannah's face and hair, but Hannah caught her arm.

"Look," she croaked.

On the broken tree branch, now coated in silver dust, lay a white fur vest, a gleaming silver bow, and a neat pile of silver arrows.

"The dwarves' gift to Dolasílla." Mom turned back to face Hannah. "You ready, Fern Hobbs?"

Hannah stared at the weapons and armor of her ancestor. She still didn't believe Spina de Mùl followed gentlemen's rules, but the

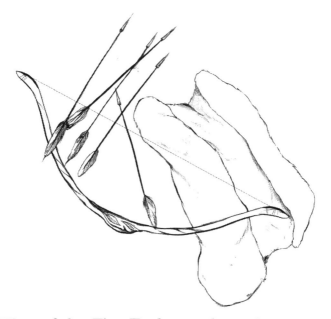

King of the Fire Eagles...at least there was a chance he might.

She nodded to her mother.

Time to get her brother back.

The white fur brushed silkily against her neck as Hannah stood next to her mother and gazed out at the clouds on the horizon. The setting sun had just begun to color them, but Hannah thought she could make out one that was unnaturally black for the hour.

And it was coming toward them.

Hannah's heart beat so fast, she had a hard time keeping hold of the heavy bow. Mom gave the zipper on Hannah's backpack a quick tug.

"I'm not sure how well the arrows will stay if you need to run. Just give it to me, if you need to, okay."

"Yeah. But what do I say to him, Mom? How...?"

Mom ran a soothing hand over Hannah's curls.

"I'll be right here beside you, my little love. But think of it like this: if they were trading sons, then they are not two separate families anymore, but one, so in a way, he is your ancestor, too."

Hannah nodded, not taking her eyes away from the approaching cloud answering her call. The cloud stopped a short distance down the trail, a greater distance in the air. Hannah glanced back at her mother who gave her a reassuring nod.

"King of the Fire Eagles!" she shouted.

The cloud responded with its dinosaur shriek.

"I wanted to apologize! I didn't recognize you when you came the first time!"

Because I'm not actually Dolasílla and you don't look anything like an eagle, you crazy brother-kidnapper!

But the hissing dinosaur sounds quieted.

"I know our families have promised to help each other."

Part of the cloud broke away. The king landed on a rough tree stump near the pond. His two friends or guards landed in the trees on either side of him. Hannah gripped the silver bow tighter in her shaky hand and stepped forward to meet him. She heard the quiet crunch of her mother's footsteps behind her.

"I'm sorry we chased you away. We don't know the stories, but we'll do our best to learn them. I know you are probably still angry—"

The guard vultures shrieked, but the king stayed quiet.

Hannah started over. "I know you are probably still angry, but we really didn't mean to hurt your feelings. Mom said that if our

SHE LOOKED THE KING RIGHT IN THE EYE.

families exchanged sons in the old days, then we aren't really two separate houses; we're one house or family or whatever you call it."

Hannah took a deep breath and looked the King of the Fire Eagles right in the eye. "So I am politely asking if you could please give my brother back. You don't need him to make sure we won't attack you. We're family."

The guards hissed and Hannah turned a glare to each of them.

"Also, in our time it is considered evil to steal a child from his family. I don't think you want to be evil bad guys, do you?"

The king hissed at his guards before they could start up again. Then he straightened and for a second, in the setting sun, Hannah could swear his bald head glowed gold with fiery feathers. He bowed gracefully to her and she carefully returned the gesture as the tails of her silver arrows tried to work loose the zipper on her backpack-quiver.

Like loosed arrows, the three birds shot into the air.

And the cloud of black feathers descended to the path.

The cloud swelled and billowed until she could see single vultures soaring up into the pinkish blue sky one by one. Then they were gone. Then there was Cameron. He stood as he had in that last glimpse she'd had, a sword-stick in one hand, his wand in the other, his backpack over both shoulders. Slowly, he seemed to come back to life, turning toward them, his eyes unfocused.

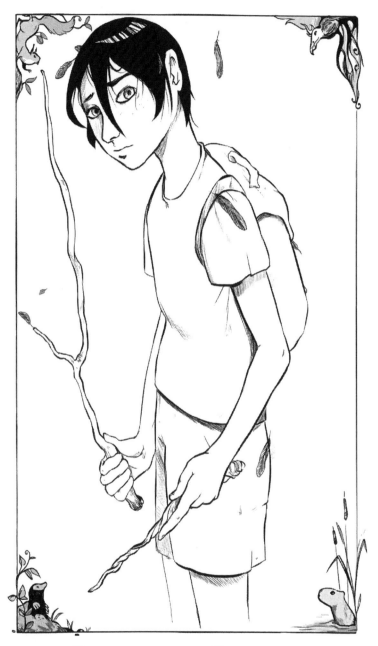

THEN THERE WAS CAMERON.

"Cameron!"

Mom rushed past Hannah and grabbed him up in her arms.

Hannah dropped the bow and the backpack full of arrows as she ran to them faster than she had ever run in her life. She threw herself at them and their arms came

around her. Cam shook in her hug, so she hugged him harder.

Mom drew back, wrapping her hands around his face.

"Are you okay? Are you hurt?"

"I'm okay. I just...it was like they turned me off. I could tell we were flying, but I couldn't see anything, I couldn't move. It was...it was so scary. How did you get me out?"

"I didn't. Your sister did." Mom glanced up at the sky. "We've got to run. They close the park gates at dusk and we are so not walking home from here. Hannah can tell you about it in the car."

She ran back and grabbed Hannah's bow and arrows. Mom's arms were full, so Hannah replaced Cam's sword-stick with her own hand

and pulled him forward. She took it as a good sign when he squeezed her hand back as they jogged together toward the parking lot.

Cam lifted his wand.

"Not really fair that they get all the magic and we get all the...nothing."

Hannah nodded back to Mom.

"Actually, we got a magic bow and arrows." She lifted the shoulder of the vest with her free hand. "And this is some kind of magic armor. I had to become a warrior to get you back."

Cam wrinkled his forehead in the dimming sun. "So do you have to fight battles now?"

Hannah's heart jumped up and smacked against her ribs as the three of them reached the parking lot where their car sat alone, waiting. Her? Fight battles? Not good. "I didn't think about that. I hope not. I won't do it. I'm not a real warrior. I just did this to get you back. I'm not a warrior."

Cam frowned as the car announced it was unlocked. Mom tossed everything in the trunk and Cam and Hannah climbed into their seats. As Mom backed the car out of the parking spot, Hannah leaned forward.

"This doesn't mean they're going to force me to be a warrior, does it, Mom?"

"Let it go, Hannah-Bannah. For now, just let it go. Right now we've got each other back and that is all that matters. I love you two. You scared me to death, but you were both so brave. And now we are going to go home and sit on the couch and eat pizza and watch a movie like totally normal people."

HAWAIIAN! SAUSAGE AND BLACK OLIVE!

"Hawaiian!" Hannah shouted.

"Sausage and black olive!" Cam called.

"Half and half it is," Mom chuckled as she pulled out onto the road.

Hannah tried to do as her mom asked and let it go, but as the car fell quiet on the ride across town, she found herself staring out her window.

And wondering.

The End
Book Two

MEET THE AUTHOR!

Tonya Macalino

lives in that space Between—where the crossroads of past and present tease the senses, taunt the almost-memory. Haunted by story, she seeks it in the shadowy landscapes of history and in the blinding glare of what-may-come, both alone and with her family of children's book authors: Raymond, Damien, & Heléna Macalino.

Need another glimpse behind the veil? Subscribe to Tonya's Reader Group at www.tonyamacalino.com for free books, guides, videos, and more! You can also drop by and chat with her on Facebook at www.facebook.com/TonyaMacalino or on Twitter @TonyaMacalino.

Got grown-ups?

Send them to Tonya's website to learn more about her national award-winning supernatural thrillers for adults, SPECTRE OF INTENTION and THE SHADES OF VENICE series!

MEET THE ARTIST!

Maya Lilova

is a humble illustrator from Sofia, Bulgaria who loves reading—and drawing—a good story. You can find her at www.mayalilova.com for an assortment of artwork or on www.facebook.com/scruffydays for a friendly chat.

Hannah and Cameron's adventure is just beginning

and so is yours!

A glimpse into the future...

Coming Fall 2017

Chapter One

A hand dropped to Hannah's shoulder.

With a groan she pushed it away. Hands, feet, and a couple of knees had thumped against her all night. She could see a crack of light between her closed eyelids. She pretended it didn't exist.

But the hand was persistent.

Again, it landed on her shoulder. This time it squeezed and shook her a little.

"Good morning, my little *schiratola*. Is this how you greet your *père*? Where are my hugs and my kisses?"

Hannah's eyes flew open.

"*Père!*"

She grabbed her father around the neck and pulled him down into the pile of arms and legs in Mom's bed that had tortured and

comforted her all night long. Dad was still wearing his jacket, belt, and shoes, so he kind of poked a lot when he landed. Hannah didn't care.

"Mphmf. Ugh, Antonio, you weigh a ton. Up, off, can't breathe!" Mom grunted in Hannah's ear.

But Cam had gotten hold of Dad's arm. Mom was doomed.

Hannah squealed as her father tickled her ribs and planted loud kisses on her cheeks, then she burrowed into her mother as Antonio turned his attack on Cam. What was another knee in the back when Daddy was finally home?

"So *mi picui morchies*, sleeping the day away, are we? I saw Ravi and Apsara outside.

They are preparing a **BBQ** tonight. Will you sleep through this as well?"

Cam dropped Dad's arm and pushed upright.

"No way! We can go, right Mom?"

"Off me!" Mom gave a huge shove that actually lifted their muscular father off the mattress. Mom was not a morning person.

Dad just laughed and sat up to kiss her on the forehead.

"*Mia doucia,* Brigida! I see you have missed me."

Mom groaned, her eyes still squinty. "You, yes. Your dragon breath and stubble, not so much."

Dad scrubbed his hand over his hair-brush-pokey baby beard. "Ey, what kind of husband visits the bathroom before his wife after such a long journey?"

"Mom, can we go?" Cam pressed again.

"Sure thing. We'll have to come up with something to make." Again with Mom the Morning Person. She sounded like she'd just agreed to attend a funeral. Hannah chuckled. *Quietly.*

"Ah, then if we are going, I must first sleep. The man in the seat next to me, he had an elbow which would not stay on his side of the armrest." Dad rubbed at his ribs. Hannah rubbed her own ribs.

"Kind of like Cam," she jibed.

"Exactly. And what is the occasion for this sleepover, anyway?" Dad's question ended on a yawn.

Suddenly, Mom's eyes were wide open. Next to Hannah, Cam stopped squirming.

"Uh," Cam replied smoothly. Hannah kicked him in the knee. He shut his mouth, but smacked her back with his hand.

"Just nightmares again," Mom said over their tussling, but Hannah saw her face twist up in a tweaky expression before she erased it with a vicious nose rub. Hannah's own face started twisting. She scrubbed her nose, too.

But Dad didn't notice. The first yawn had turned into a series of yawns that had his eyes squeezed tight shut. He just nodded as he stumbled toward the bedroom door and to the bathroom he had skipped on the way in.

Hannah, Cameron, and Bridget all lay perfectly still under the covers until they heard the bathroom door slam closed. Then in a rustle of sheets they sat up. Hannah looked first to her brother, then her mother.

They sat frozen in a long, thick, icky silence.

Mom was the first to move. She dropped her face into her hands.

"Oh, muffin mittens, I have no idea what to tell him."

Hannah turned her gaze back to Cam.

HE'S NEVER GOING TO BELIEVE US.

Blue Bathrobe Man, royal squirrels, kidnapping vultures, a magic bow and arrow, and an armor of white fur?

Cam just shook his head.

"He's never going to believe us."

Tonya would like to thank:

The talented and lovely Maya Lilova, the artist whose work graces these pages!

Thanks go to her editors Damien Macalino, Trixy Buttcane, Shannon Page, and Raymond Macalino who make it possible for her to communicate coherently with the outside world.

And to the kind and welcoming community of Hillsboro, Oregon, for sharing the inspiring secrets of its past.

And, of course, she would like to thank her family, Raymond, Damien, & Heléna Macalino, who gave her the time and opportunity to scheme great schemes.

Thanks

Maya would like to thank:

My partner, family, and friends who have enabled me to be who I am;

My various pets who constantly remind me;

And the masterful Tonya Macalino who has given me the wonderful opportunity to take part in this great adventure!

Collect all 10 Books!

The Gates of AURONA

BOOK I
The Gates of
AURONA
INTO THE
HARE WOOD
TONYA MACALINO • MAYA LILOVA

BOOK II
The Gates of
AURONA
THE
ANGUANA'S
TALE
TONYA MACALINO • MAYA LOVA

BOOK III
The Gates of
AURONA
SPINWATCH
TONYA MACALINO • MAYA LILOVA

#4
Spirits
of the
Silver Screen

#5
The
Curse of the
Children

#6
The
Gates of
Auròna

#7
The
Battle at
Five Oaks

#8
Heroes and
Legends of
Hillsboro

#9
The
Kingdom of
The Fànes

The Gates of
AURONA
CREATURES
OF THE
DOLOMITES

Check **www.TonyaMacalino.com** for release dates.

Made in the USA
Columbia, SC
01 November 2017